Translated by Sarah Gibson

©1988 by Bohem Press
First published in Great Britain in 1989 by Andersen Press Ltd., 62-65 Chandos Place,
London WC2N 4NW. Published in Australia by Century Hutchinson Pty. Ltd., 89-91
Albion Street, Surry Hills, NSW 2010. This translation ©1989 by Andersen Press Ltd.
All rights reserved. Original title: *An einem schönen Sommertag.*
Printed in Italy.

One Fine Day in Summertime

Text by Max Bolliger
Pictures by Jindra Čapek

Andersen Press · London
Hutchinson · Australia

One fine day in summertime
on a meadow in the forest
a fox and a raven,
a tortoise and a hare,
a peacock and a crow
and a wolf and a dog
met up together.

The sun shone down.
The animals decided to hold a celebration feast.
There was plenty to eat and plenty to drink.
The peacock spread his tail in a fan.
The raven and the crow croaked out a song.

The fox and the tortoise,
the hare and the wolf
danced to the music as best they could.

There was joy and happiness between them
in spite of all their differences.

As evening drew on and the sun went down
they fell on the idea of story telling.

The first to step forward was the fox
and he told this fable

The Fox and the Raven

A raven once stole a piece of cheese and was sitting on the branch of a tree feeling very pleased with himself.

But before he had a chance to enjoy his prize, a fox came up the road. He had smelled the cheese from a long way off and was determined to have it.

'Good evening, Sir Raven!' he began politely.

The raven was holding the cheese in his beak, so gave no reply.

'How beautiful you look today!' the fox went on. 'Your feathers are gleaming like a peacock's. And as for your eyes! They sparkle like two precious stones!'

The raven began to twist and turn under this flattery.

'But it's your beak that I admire the most,' continued the fox. 'Your voice must truly be beyond compare. If only I could hear it just once!'

His head swimming with the fox's words, the raven opened his beak and began to croak for all he was worth.

The cheese fell to the ground.

The fox snatched it up and trotted off, laughing.

As the fox
came to the end of his story,
all the animals
began to laugh—
all, that is, except the raven.
'That served the raven right!'
they shouted.

But the raven
could think of nothing else
but how
he could get his revenge on the fox.

Next the tortoise stepped forward
and told this fable

The Tortoise and the Hare

There was once a boastful hare who kept on
bragging about how fast he could run.
One day he met a tortoise.
When he saw her short little legs he began to
 laugh at her.
The tortoise was not the least bit bothered.
'Let's have a race,' she suggested.
'Gladly!' scoffed the hare. 'I'm sure you'll beat me!'
They agreed on a winning post and set off.
The hare streaked away, not taking the race seriously
at all.
At the halfway mark, he lay down in the grass. The
tortoise was nowhere to be seen.
I could easily take a little nap, he thought, and still
win the race.
But the tortoise plodded on steadily, never once
stopping even for a moment.
And when the hare woke up and ran off again, the
tortoise had already reached the winning post and
was waiting for him.

As the tortoise
came to the end of her story,
all the animals
began to laugh—
all, that is, except the raven
and the hare.
'That served the hare right!'
they shouted.

But the hare
sat down beside the raven
and could think of nothing else
but how he could get his revenge on the tortoise.

Then the peacock stepped forward
and told this fable

The Peacock and the Crow

There was once a vain crow who despised her own kind and was never happy with her looks.

One day she found some feathers which had fallen from a peacock.

'These are just what I need,' she said to herself, and she began to dress up in them.

When she was satisfied that no one would recognise her, she began to mingle with a group of peacocks.

But those beautiful birds were not to be deceived.

With harsh cries they fell on the crow and plucked the false feathers from her.

'Stop! Leave me alone!' cried the crow.

There she stood in her jet black plumage, just as she was meant to be.

But when the peacocks saw her gleaming black feathers, they said: 'Surely those don't belong to you either!'

And they pecked at the crow until all but a few of her feathers lay at her feet.

As the peacock
came to the end of her story,
all the animals
began to laugh—
all, that is, except the raven,
the hare and the crow.
'That served the crow right!'
they shouted.

But the crow
sat down beside the hare and the raven
and could think of nothing else
but how she could get her revenge on the peacock.

Then the wolf stepped forward
and told this fable

The Wolf and the Dog

There was once a wolf who was so hungry that his ribs stood out from his body.

It was winter.

He was searching for food and on his way he met a sleek and well-fed dog.

'I'm stronger than you,' said the wolf, 'and yet I'm nearly dying of hunger. How come you're so plump?'

The dog was flattered and replied: 'If you carried out the same duties for my master as I do, you could do just as well. As many bones and chunks of meat as you like, and a full stomach without a great deal of effort.'

'What sort of duties are they?' asked the wolf.

'I guard the gate and protect the farm from thieves,' answered the dog. 'Come with me!'

In snow and bitter weather like this, thought the wolf, even a wolf might do well to live indoors.

But as they trotted along side by side, the wolf noticed a festering sore on the dog's neck.

'How did you get that wound?' he asked.

'Oh, it's nothing,' said the dog.

But the wolf repeated the question and finally the dog answered in a dejected voice:

'It comes from the chain my master uses to tie me up.'

'Then you can keep your food,' said the wolf. 'I would rather go hungry and be my own master.'

As the wolf
came to the end of his story,
all the animals
began to laugh—
all, that is, except the raven,
the hare, the crow
and the dog.
'That served the dog right!'
they shouted.

But the dog
sat down beside the crow,
the hare and the raven,
and could think of nothing else
but how he could get his revenge on the wolf.

Then the fox, the tortoise,
the peacock and the wolf
stopped laughing.
They stood face to face
with the dog, the crow,
the hare and the raven,
who could think of nothing else
but how to get their revenge.

And they began to fight,
at first with words
and then with blows
and bites and scratches.

The beautiful clearing
turned into a battlefield.
At times one side seemed
to be winning,
at times the other seemed
to take the upper hand.

Nearby
a wise old lion
was sleeping.
Woken by the noise
he stood up to see
what all the rumpus was about.

When the fighting animals
saw the lion,
they fell silent.
Even the wolf
began to tremble with fear.

The lion wanted to know
why they had been fighting.
So the raven and the hare,
the crow and the dog
told him
how the fox and the tortoise,
the peacock and the wolf
had jeered at them.

The lion listened carefully,
and then he also told
a story.
The lion told his fable.

The Lion and the Mouse

One hot midday a lion lay down to sleep.
A mouse scampered over his gigantic paws and
woke him up.
Furious at being disturbed, the lion seized the tiny
creature and was about to eat him.
But the mouse pleaded with him. 'King of Beasts,
you are used to grappling with bulls and stags. I
would only be a tiny mouthful for you. Spare me, I
beg you. Perhaps one day I shall be able to repay
you.'
The lion laughed at such impudence but allowed the
mouse to go free.
Not long afterwards, the lion found himself caught
in the net of a hunter. Desperately he tried to free
himself, but only managed to become more
entangled in the mesh.
Woken by his roaring, the mouse came out of his
hole, and immediately ran to help. He gnawed away
at the cords of the net and did not stop until the lion
was free.

As the lion
came to the end of his story,
a little mouse crept out of his hole.
He had been watching
and listening
to everything that had happened.
Now he began to squeak
with delight.

The other animals
thought about the fable
the lion had told them,
and gradually
they understood what it meant.

They made peace with one another
and the celebrations
continued till dawn.
The fox danced with the raven,
the tortoise with the hare,
the peacock with the crow,
the wolf with the dog,
and, of course,
the lion with the little mouse.